MW01009521

Gabriel's Big Announcement

Luke 1-2, Retold for Children

Holli Fry

Illustrated by
Elena Komarova

Gabriel's Big Announcement
(Luke 1-2 Retold for Children)

Copyright © 2021 by Holli Fry
All rights reserved.

Written by Holli Fry
Illustrated by Elena Komarova
Edited by Lesa Pepper
Author photo by Cargil Photography of Uvalde, TX

"Something big is about to happen," said Gabriel to his friend.
"I have an important job to do: I'm going to descend
To Earth and tell some news about a little baby boy.
His parents are going to be surprised and shout and clap for joy!"

"His father's in the temple now, so, quickly, I must go.
Now's the time—the perfect time—to let this family know:
Their son, born oh-so-late in their lives, is a very special man,
Sent to reveal to all the earth God's oh-so-glorious plan."

Leaning out over the edge of the boat and seeing his own reflection,
Gabriel thought, "I'll scare them to death before even one interjection!"
Then he remembered the most important words a big angel should know:
"Fear not! Fear not!" He said them aloud and kept his voice calm and low.

Turning toward his friend in the boat, he said, "I think I'm ready!
Reel in the lines! No more fishing today, just turn around slow and steady.
Use those big muscles of yours to the max and pick up your golden oar!"
With sudden impatience, he bellowed, "Michael, row the boat ashore!"

Reaching the bank of the Emerald Sea, Gabriel hurried away.
Knowing the weight of the message he bore gave him strength to fly that day.
He couldn't wait to complete the task. The words he would say were unknown,
But he felt that he was about to lay an important cornerstone.

After completing the job that God had sent him off to do,
Gabriel hurried back to his friend to tell him what was new.
Searching high and low, he finally saw him gathering wheat.
(In the fertile fields of heaven, there's always plenty to eat.)

"Michael! I met Zechariah!" he shouted, "the father-to-be of John!
And John is the prophet whom God will send to prepare the earth for His son!
He is the one who is going to bring the people back to the Lord!
Wisdom and righteousness will return, and families will live in accord!"

"Amazing!" his soft-spoken friend replied as he tied up a bundle of wheat.
"But did he believe you?" Michael asked as he plucked some grain to eat.
"Of course not," Gabriel said with a grin, "so I had to make him mute,
Until the baby is born, of course. Then he can holler and hoot."

Thinking a great deal of time would pass before he was summoned again,
Gabriel busied himself with gathering grapes out in the glen.
    Yet only six months by Earth's odd way of counting were completed;
The angel was quite beside himself when he was again entreated!

THIS time he was going to see the mother of God's own Son!
What an amazing thing it would be to announce the Holy One!
Leaving his basket behind, he ran as fast as his legs could go,
Then flew like a mighty eagle down to tiny Earth below.

Finding Mary in a town by the Sea of Galilee,
He knew she had to be the one that he'd been sent to see:
Betrothed to Joseph, descended from David, a virgin, according to plan.
"You're going to have a baby," he said, "although you've known no man."

Seeing her look of dread, he remembered his most important words:
"Fear not! Fear not!" He said them soft, like the coo of the morning birds.
Then he continued, seeing that she was ready to hear the rest:
"Your child will be the Son of God, the highest and the best.

"His reign will last forever, His kingdom never end,
And you will name Him 'Jesus,' the lowly to defend."
"I'm the Lord's servant," the maiden cried. "May it be to me as you've said."
And then the angel flew away, his glorious wings outspread.

The day that baby John was born, Gabe was so excited.
He watched from Heaven, for, you see, to Earth, he wasn't invited.
List'ning with bated breath, he wondered what Zachariah would say.
Having been silent for almost a year, would he prophesy or pray?

When the man spoke for the very first time since a hush that was oh-so-long,
His heart was full, his message clear, his voice was loud and strong:
"You, my child, will be the prophet proclaiming the Lord Most High!
You will tell the people about salvation by-and-by.

"'The rising sun shall come to us from heaven,' you'll proclaim,
'Shining in the darkness like a never-ending flame,
Leading us out of the shadow of death and guiding our feet to peace,
Bringing salvation from our sins, and the mercies of God shall not cease!'"

There was singing and dancing and feasting and gladness in Heaven on that day,
But Gabriel knew a more glorious birth was about to come his way!
The Son of God would soon be born into the human race,
In Bethlehem, a tiny town; who's heard of such a place?

When that day came, the angels obediently took their assigned position,
Where they could watch what happened below; it was their supposition,
That they were not allowed to go and make an angelic appearance.
Surely that would be to all the folks an interference.

But suddenly Gabriel heard the call to fly to Earth below!
The other angels heard it too! They ALL were going to go!
They hurried and scurried and flurried about, fluffing their hair and their wings!
"How like humans we are," Gabe thought, "worrying about all these things!"

Yet there was no more time for this because, on lowly Earth,
Some shepherds were waiting in the field so near the holy birth.
They would want to hear the news so they could go and see,
For this was truly an event—a cause for jubilee!

So Gabriel flew ahead of the rest and appeared in the sky glowing bright,
Above the shepherds, who fell upon the ground and trembled with fright.
"Fear not! Fear not!" He began with the words he had practiced o'er and o'er.
"I bring you good news of great joy for all the people from shore to shore."

"Today in the town of Bethlehem, a Savior has been born!
And He is Christ the Lord, the glorious Star of early morn!
This shall be your sign: In a manger you will find him,
Wrapped in swaddling clothes—the sheep and goats behind him."

Suddenly, a great company of the heavenly host appeared,
Singing, "Glory to God in the highest! The Savior now is here!
Peace on Earth! Goodwill to men on whom His favor rests.
For God has chosen this very night His love to manifest!"

Then almost as quickly as they had arrived, the angels all departed.
They had done what they came to do. Their message was now imparted.
But Gabriel tarried a moment longer, his eyes full of wonder,
Watching the shepherds proceed toward the little town down under.

All of a sudden, he saw the One his heart was yearning for –
The tiny babe, the Son of God, the Holy One, the Lord,
Lying in a manger, wrapped in swaddling, as foretold,
The smile on His face more precious than rubies, more glorious than gold!

Winging his way back to Heaven, he found his friends
    in glad celebration.
Michael, the normally quiet one, was singing in exultation!
A feast was served—fish, bread, and wine,
And all the angels sat to dine.

But as the food was passed around,
Gabriel had a thought profound:
"What's the meaning of bread and wine?
Is this a sacrifice divine?

"Has God sent down His only Son
To Earth, for all mankind to shun?
Was this baby born to die—
The very Apple of God's eye?"

Gabe knew it was so, and here is why:

"For God—so loved—the world."

Seeing now what God had planned,
Gabriel held the cup in his hand,
And began to sing a song so glorious
That all the angels joined the chorus:

"Holy, holy, holy, Lord!
You above all else adored!
May your people always raise
Their voices in eternal praise!"

About the Author

    As Holli Fry raised her family, she found herself frequently searching for books that would bring her children closer to God, either by retelling Bible stories in a child-friendly way or through imaginative fiction that encourages Christian values. She and her husband spent many an evening reading to their children. They still enjoy this activity with their rapidly-growing host of grandchildren. Hoping to add to the selection of quality Christian literature for children, Holli recently published her first book, *Amena's Quest,* an allegorical middle-grade novel about a young girl and her search for the king.

    Holli is now proud to announce the first of a series of Bible stories retold in rhyming verse and beautifully illustrated to bring them to life for children. *Gabriel's Big Announcement,* the first of this series, narrates the events surrounding the birth of Jesus, as related in Luke 1-2, using lively verse and fun imagery.

    You are invited to visit Holli's web site at www.hollifrybooks.com to follow the progress of her books, both published and "in process." Within the web site, be sure and submit your email address so you may join her newsletter group and receive ongoing updates about her publications.